Good Things from Farms

Written by Catherine Baker

Collins

Lots of things come from farms.

The crops on this farm will turn into all sorts of food!

This crop is oats. Oats have long stems.

oats

We mix the oats into flapjacks.

flapjacks

Milk from cows turns into butter.

We drink milk, too!

This crop is corn. We munch it for dinner.

We get electric power from this farm!

The panels turn light from the sun into power.

Light from the sun hits the panels.

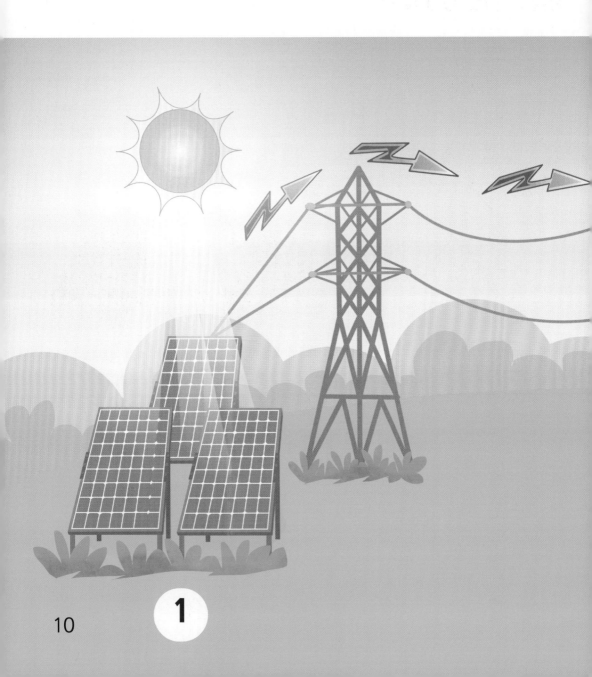

1

The panels can turn the light into electric power.

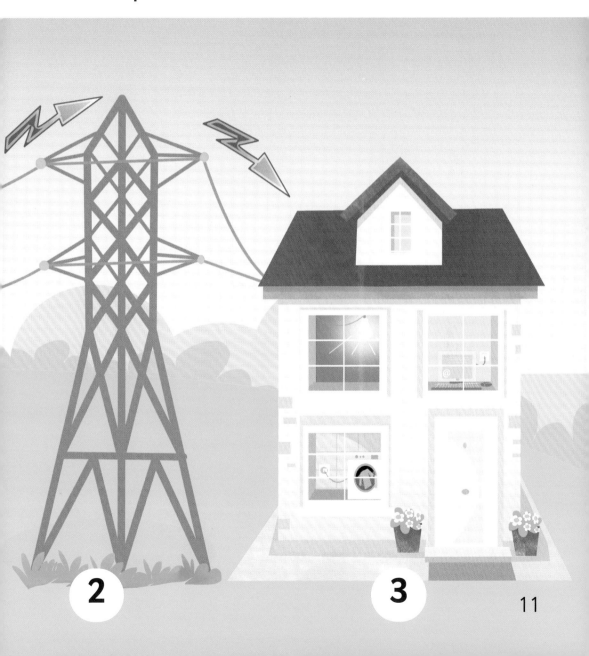

2

3

Power from farms helps us do lots of things.

It can light up electric bulbs!

Crops

Electric power

After reading

Letters and Sounds: Phase 4

Word count: 100

Focus on adjacent consonants with short vowel phonemes, e.g. *crops*

Common exception words: of, the, into, all, we, have, do, come

Curriculum links: Understanding the world

Curriculum links (National Curriculum, Year 1): Human and physical geography; Design and technology

Early learning goals: Reading: read and understand simple sentences; use phonic knowledge to decode regular words and read them aloud accurately; read some common irregular words

National Curriculum learning objectives: Reading/word reading: read accurately by blending sounds in unfamiliar words containing GPCs that have been taught; Reading/comprehension: understand both the books they can already read accurately and fluently and those they listen to by checking that the text makes sense to them as they read, and correcting inaccurate reading

Developing fluency

- Encourage your child to follow the words as you read the first pages with expression, asking your child to make sure you are reading words correctly.
- Take turns to read a page, encouraging your child to read the sentences that end with an exclamation mark with surprise or extra enthusiasm.

Phonic practice

- Practise reading words that contain adjacent consonants. Encourage your child to sound out and blend the following:

  stems   crops   munch   from   hits   things

- Focus on multi-syllable words. Check your child includes all the sounds, for example check they do not miss "t" in **electric**.

  flapjacks   dinner   panels   butter   power

Extending vocabulary

- Challenge your child to think of a word or words with a similar meaning to the following. Ask them to reread the page first to check the context.

  page 3: turn into (e.g. *make, produce*)   page 7: munch (e.g. *nibble, eat*)
  page 10: hits (e.g. *reaches, touches*)
- Does each replacement make sense in the sentences?